SAFE! in OUTERSPACE

ANITA *and* BRANDON HOLMES

illustrated by

ANTONIO PAHETTI

BIBLIOKID
PUBLISHING

"For all those 'This one time
when I was a baby in a carrier' stories."

I was asleep in my bed when...

CRASH! An alien spaceship landed in my room.

"Brandon, we need your help! Our star player just got hurt. Hurry up and get in before we miss the game," the alien explained.

"What game? I can't go into space!" I said.
But he ignored me.

"Let's go," he said.
I climbed in the spaceship.
(He was stealing my bed
after all.)

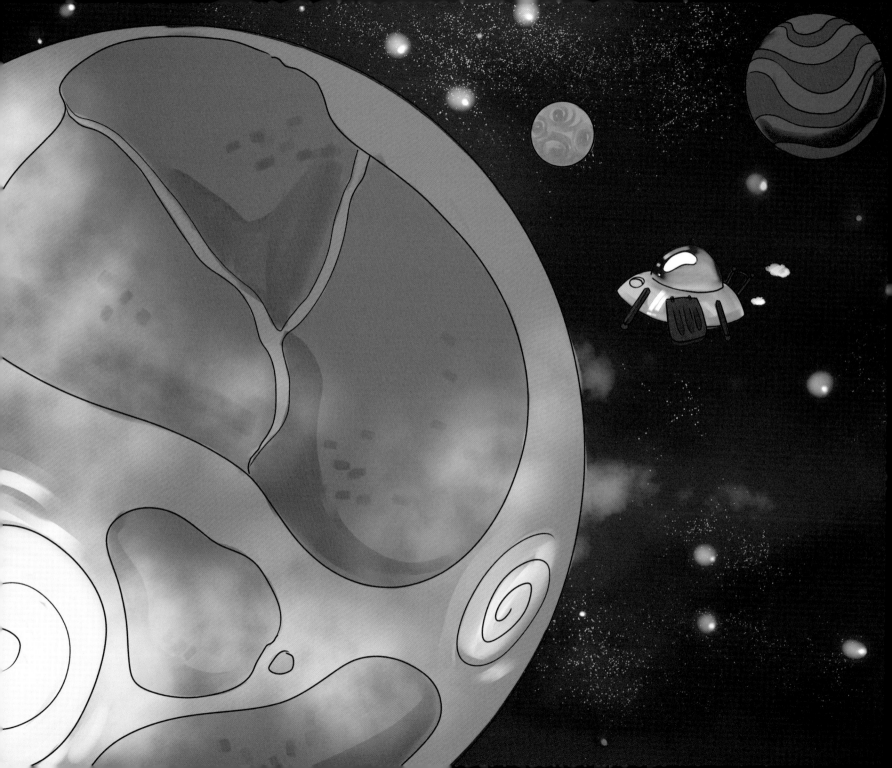

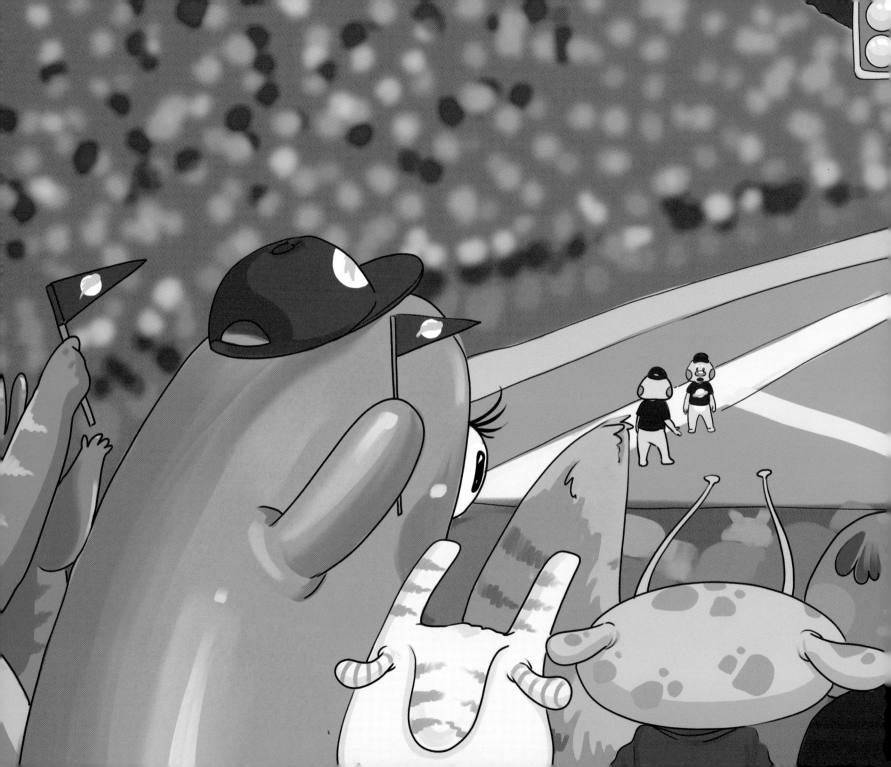

It wasn't like any baseball game I had ever played before.

The aliens helped me put on a jetpack.

I'd never used one before but how hard could it be?

It was a lot harder than I thought.

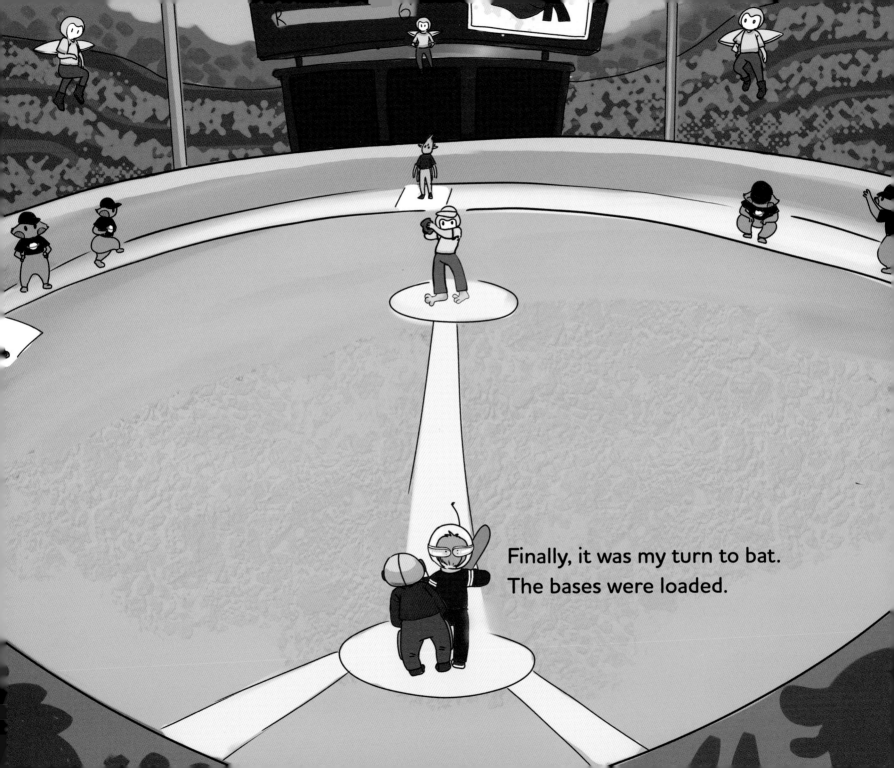

Finally, it was my turn to bat.
The bases were loaded.

The pitcher threw the ball and...

He pitched a backward curveball and...
STRIKE TWO!

The team was counting on me.
I couldn't let them down. The next pitch
was a high loop-de-loop.
I swung and...

As I rounded third base, their outfielder picked up the ball. The catcher readied himself at the plate.

I slid just as the ball smacked into his glove

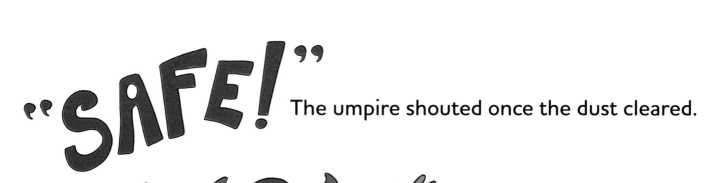

"**SAFE!**" The umpire shouted once the dust cleared.

We'd won the game!

After the celebration, I asked the alien if he could take me home.

It was starting to get late, and
I didn't want my mom to be worried.

We landed back in my room just as the sun was rising. As I waved goodbye, I realized he still had my bed! Then I heard footsteps...

I panicked. How was I going to explain what happened to my bed?

The door creaked open and Mom stuck her head inside...

I launched into a full explanation of everything that had happened. "Sounds like you had a fun dream last night," she said and kissed the top of my head.

I spun around and saw my room exactly how it had been before the alien arrived.

Had it all been a dream?